BROWNIE & PEARL

See the Sights

by CYNTHIA RYLANT ✿ pictures by BRIAN BIGGS

Beach Lane Books

New York London Toronto Sydney

**Brownie and Pearl
are off to see the sights.**

Brownie has her handbag.
Pearl has her mouse.
They look very smart.

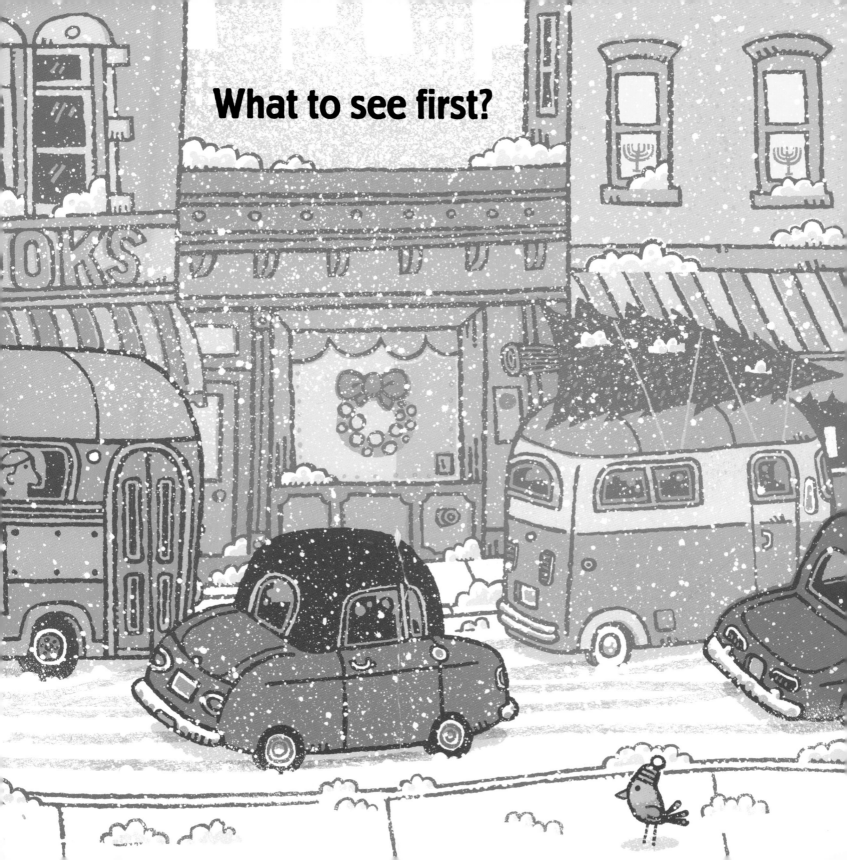

What to see first?

The hat shop.

Brownie **loves** hats.

Pearl does too.

What next?

The shoe shop.

Brownie loves shoes.

Pearl does too.

Now what?

The cupcake shop.

Everybody loves cupcakes!

Brownie has a big bite.
Pearl has a little bite.

Then Brownie yawns.
Pearl does too.

Cupcakes and sights
have made them sleepy.

Brownie gets her handbag.
Pearl gets her mouse.

Home they go.
To nap.
Together.

Sights are good . . .

but home is better.

For my mom
—B. B.

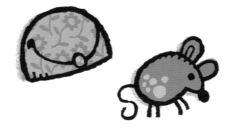

BEACH LANE BOOKS
An imprint of Simon & Schuster Children's Publishing Division
1230 Avenue of the Americas, New York, New York 10020
Text copyright © 2010 by Cynthia Rylant
Illustrations copyright © 2010 by Brian Biggs
All rights reserved, including the right of reproduction in whole or in part in any form.
BEACH LANE BOOKS is a trademark of Simon & Schuster, Inc.
For information about special discounts for bulk purchases, please contact Simon & Schuster Special Sales
at 1-866-506-1949 or business@simonandschuster.com.
The Simon & Schuster Speakers Bureau can bring authors to your live event. For more information or to book an event,
contact the Simon & Schuster Speakers Bureau at 1-866-248-3049 or visit our website at www.simonspeakers.com.
Book design by Sonia Chaghatzbanian
The text for this book is set in Berliner Grotesk.
The illustrations for this book are rendered digitally.
Manufactured in China
0310 SCP
First Edition
2 4 6 8 10 9 7 5 3 1
Library of Congress Cataloging-in-Publication Data
Rylant, Cynthia.
Brownie & Pearl see the sights / Cynthia Rylant ; illustrated by Brian Biggs.—1st ed.
p. cm.
Summary: After visiting the shoe shop, the hat shop, and the cupcake shop, a weary little girl and her sleepy cat head home for a nap.
ISBN 978-1-4169-8637-9 (hardcover : alk. paper)
[1. Cats—Fiction. 2. Shopping—Fiction.] I. Biggs, Brian, ill. II. Title. III. Title: Brownie and Pearl see the sights.
PZ7.R982Bs 2010
[E]—dc22
2009012577